Archways 1

Published in the United States by:
Archway Editions,
a division of powerHouse Cultural Entertainment, Inc.
32 Adams Street, Brooklyn, NY 11201

www.archwayeditions.us

Daniel Power, CEO
Chris Molnar, Editorial Director
Nicodemus Nicoludis, Managing Editor
Naomi Falk, Editor

Library of Congress Control Number: 2020950785

ISBN 978-1-57687-975-7

Printed by Toppan Leefung

First edition, 2023

10 9 8 7 6 5 4 3 2 1

Interior layout and design by Robert Avellan with Chris Molnar

Printed and bound in China

ARCHWAY
EDITIONS

Archways 1

**Edited by Chris Molnar
and Nicodemus Nicoludis**

Archway Editions, Brooklyn, NY

CONTENTS

INTRODUCTION

In 2020 Archway Editions published *Unpublishable*, a collection of works read at POWERHOUSE Arena's reading series of the same name. An outgrowth of the Ungallery series at Columbia University's School of the Arts, Unpublishable was designed as a space for writers to try out their wildest ideas—"writing that excites you, that scares you, things that you delete from your browser history. The piece you can't submit but can't stop thinking about either, burning a hole in the bottom of your desk drawer. Writing from any genre that is uncharacteristic, outré, or offending of sensibilities, that is impossible to place or be published in some fashion." Each event came with a chapbook of the works read therein, and the book collected them—urgent, unique, uncompromised work by major writers like Jean Kyoung Frazier, Jameson Fitzpatrick, Steve Anwyll, and Arash Azizi.

The Archways reading series is the successor to that—tied directly into the Archway Editions imprint of powerHouse Books, begun by Arena booksellers Chris Molnar and Nicodemus Nicoludis as a pipeline from the edges to the center, made possible by distribution from a "Big Five" (now "Big Four") publisher Simon & Schuster. *Archways* takes the Unpublishable ethos (against the mainstream, genre-blind, inclusive even of photography and film) and tries to explicitly make it a farm league of writers to watch. This is a compilation of the first three events, the third of which happened to have been planned for March 14, 2020 and so is still being delayed, possibly forever, a permanent floating invisible event that will always and never be taking place. We'll take that as a sign of some sort—*Archways* was born into fire, or destined to be a light in dark times, or some other bright and improbably positive metaphor.

The idea for *Archways* came from thinking of how to get Naomi Falk's writing in front of you. Her work—you'll read it here—is dense, allusive, beautiful, rich with feeling. The sort of thing that a cult of devoted readers would cherish from an august experimental writer. But how does anyone become that niche, august figure? Our first book was *The Haunting of Lin-Manuel Miranda* by Ishmael Reed (who is also publishing *Life Among the Aryans* with us later this year, with more on the horizon), and he's a perfect example. He co-founded the *East Village Other*, and joined Umbra Writers Workshop and the Black Arts Movement, before moving out West and founding *Yardbird*, Konch, the Before Columbus Foundation, the American Book Awards, and inspiring other legendary groups like the Combined Asian American Resources Project, which came together at a party he held in 1970 to celebrate *19 Necromancers From Now*—a compilation of yet another grouping of writers resolutely on the periphery that Ishmael wanted to bring the world's attention to. In *Necromancers*, authors from Reed's milieu are placed next to each other, the conventional and the totally out-there, united not by form but by their marginal nature and their stance against the establishment. This is how we could do it, how we could elevate writers from the contemporary periphery. Build a series, build a context, build a scene.

As you can see from Ishmael's career, outside the mainstream is where the *scene* has to happen. And outside the current milieu of publishing, hinged on commercially successful, corporate-sanctioned writing which produces more light than heat. But how do you get people on the street to actually *read* work by new writers, particularly those working out of the mainstream, those who want to change culture, not obey it? How do you get interested people to come out and listen? Unpublishable had run its course—all good things should end, especially if that ending is an impromptu poetry reading under the Manhattan Bridge Archway. So, we were back to doing an event series, which was the one ace we had up our sleeves—working in a giant bookstore in the heart of Brooklyn. This time we had Ki Smith Gallery up in Harlem printing luxurious limited edition chapbooks (instead of Chris stealing printing money through a complex scam involving tech support up at Columbia's Butler Library and binding them together with Nick's saddle-stich stapler) and a project-based mission.

We've already published the entirety of Gabriel Kruis' astounding *Acid Virga* (Archway Editions, 2020), a memoir-in-verse in the tradition of the greats like Eileen Myles or Alice Notley, whose epic blurb we carried like a totem in front to promote it, and whose *Runes and Chords* we are publishing this year. But Gabe is just the beginning of a host of writers whose work shook our reading series to the core. We have a short, searing piece by Cyree Jarelle Johnson, whose *Slingshot* (Nightboat, 2019) was one of the best poetry debuts of the past few years. Joseph Rathgeber's anti-publishing manifesto shocked the literary establishment elements at the second Archways event. Appropriately enough, you won't find that here as we are true believers in the *physical*, in the improvised chaos of a hothouse non-Zoom *performance*, but here we present the poems from the legendary proprietor of Radical Paper Press—his all-stolen materials, all-free chapbooks concern that was too good to live.

We also present to you work from erstwhile POWERHOUSE employees (Katie Foster), work that speaks to us right now, (Kwame Opoku-Duku telling us "politics bought status in the land of the incorruptible") and work that speaks to the end of time ("the only thing in the world that's worth beginning: the end of the world" says Ariel Francisco), and much else. That's not to mention more *Draft Dodgers* from *Unpublishable* co-editor Etan Nechin, his subtly radical generational study of running away from war, or Andrea Stella's vivid East Village vignettes from the first Archways, a perfect complement to Brendan Burdzinski's Tompkins Square Park photos which serve as the cover here and another encapsulation of our de-gentrification ethos, of a reading series and bookstore and publishing imprint unapologetically based in late-capitalist New York City, proud to say this is the greatest city in the world with the richest culture, bar none.

We are here to break windows, lower rents and antagonize received convention, not to collaborate with the invidious tech and investment firms that are destroying America's cities with cultural sanitization, diseased whiteness, unaffordability, and Edison bulbs. We are here to pursue a writing, a scene, free from cops and landlords, free from predatory agents and the Market of Books that created them and the writers who strive to be spoken for by them. New York is the center of that scene because this scene was built from it; it was built from an intensity, beauty, history, or infrastructure unlike anywhere else right now. Or so we humbly submit.

The writers who are in print here are the true writers of tomorrow, with ambitions literary, not monetary, all karmically linked through a bookstore in Brooklyn. We are humbled to have been able to host them or to have dreamt of hosting them in simpler times, by which we mean 2019 and 2020, the last years of innocence before we all became adults whether we wanted to or not, when restive ideals (or lack thereof) were forced into the open and the words had to hit the page.

Here they are.

Kwame Opoku-Duku

politics

bought status in the land
of the incorruptible/ & a
backscratcher with gail
devers' fingernails/ as you
close your eyes & push the
button/ take off your veil &
get that look up off your face/
be cooler than duke ellington
on a swedish night/ take mdma
& see the prison camps for your-
self/ be cooler than duke ellington
on a swedish night/ satisfy that
man in uniform fantasy/ lest we
forget the names of our most
masculine brothers/ lest we
succumb to the devils in the
dim fluorescence of a parking
garage/ if you want this
work my nigga i'll give
it to you/ just take off that
veil & get that look up off
your face/ be cooler than duke
ellington on a swedish night/
as close your eyes & push the
button/ i'll scratch your back
with lee press on nails/ bought
status in the land of authenticity

sonnet for the day of the lord

you will be in your living room, singing melismas.
everything you utter is a prayer. your tears
water the lush earth as an offering to the lord.
from out of nowhere, a Chevy Caprice pulls up,
the windows roll down, St. Michael starts blasting.
in a drawn-out falsetto, he sings, *the day of the Lord
is a bitter motherlover.* you look out the window.
the world is on fire. every moment is spent on your knees.
everything you utter is a prayer. *dona novis pacem.*
out of nowhere, a Chevy Caprice pulls up, Michael
starts blasting. everybody hits the floor. the Caprice
pulls away, Mike's falsetto rings: *if you think you're
holy now, baby, wait until tonight.* it feels good when
you cry out. your battered lungs wail a soulful tune.

Katie Foster

I feel a little bit insane sitting on the couch in the middle of the afternoon. I'm never home at this hour. The apartment looks unfamiliar to me. Light comes in from the window over by the bookshelf, making a rectangle on the floor that tracks across the room all day. I alternate between watching the rectangle of light on the floor and the rectangle of light in my hand.

68,320, 70,003, 77,336. 82,000. 85,484, 86,240, 89,992. 91,000, 93,304.

The rectangle of light starts to climb the far wall when I realize I haven't eaten anything since Rodger left this morning. I grunt, stuffing my device between the couch cushions to muffle any vibrations.

When I walk to the kitchen, I feel like a bootleg stream of a movie still in theaters, audio track off a fraction of a second from the action of the film. Mind lagging behind body. Everything in the kitchen looks bright and beautiful. It hurts my eyes. I have a headache. I don't know what I want to eat and the prospect of figuring out what to put in my body makes my head hurt more. I microwave a bowl of oatmeal. As I watch the dish spin behind meshed glass, I regret my choice - the milk froths, the mixture bubbles, it looks so unappetizing that I have to go sit down. A half step before I make it back to the couch, I slice open my foot.

The pain jolts me back into my body, mind right where it should be, focused on the shard of glass sticking out of my foot and the blood, blood on the glass and my foot and the rug, soaking beneath into the cracks of the hardwood, on my hands, under my nails, in my hair as I try to push it out of my face.

I tug the shard of glass free from my flesh with a disgusting squelch, the sound making me shiver more than the sensation. Blood on the couch as I dig between the cushions for my device. I call Rodger crying. At first he thinks I'm upset over the upload.

"What is it, Tilly, trolls, already?"

"Rodger, no, my foot - it's my fucking foot, I stepped on glass," I spit.

I break 200,000 views just after I've been stitched up. I sit back, holding my device to my chest, feeling damp beneath the horrible hospital lights.

———

My father builds a house for me and Rodger. The ceilings are high, almost out of sight, with windows way up there, light drifting down, barely reaching us, walls made of rough adobe. I run my hands over them, palms tingling. Two little girls dart in and out of adjacent rooms. I assume these are my daughters. My daughters with Rodger.

The entrance is a large double door made of glass. People keep coming in, looking around, looking like they're looking for business and I can't blame them, the doors seem like they belong on a bank or a library. I redirect the lost back outside. This is our home! You can't come in! I try to write a sign to post on the door, but the letters dissolve as soon as I put them to page.

Rodger's weirded out by the daughters.

"Do you want kids? I thought you said you didn't want kids?" he says, a sharp note in his voice like he's scared.

"No, no, Rodger, it was just a dream," I say, raising my hands like I'm innocent. "Have you ever had dreams about kids before? Like, having kids?" he asks.

"I barely remembered dreams before all this started," I say, "But I guess the girls did feel familiar, like I knew them, and that's how I understood they were my daughters, I felt like I knew them. Or maybe I'd seen them before," I say. "Maybe I've seen them in real life and adopted them into my dreams."

"You're dreaming about other people's kids?" Rodger asks, even more weirded out.

"No! I mean, yes, maybe. But not like, stealing kids," I say, "Obviously." Rodger gives me a strange, long look.

"What?" I ask.

"Nothing," he says. "I was just thinking. If it's art."

"If it's art, Rodger," I say, "it might mean something, but that doesn't make it real."

———

My dad calls. My dad never calls. It's always mom. It's always mom and dad's in the background doing stuff. My heart ticks hard when I pick up the call.

"Dad, what's up?" I say.

Before he speaks I can tell he's crying. "Oh, Tilly, it's horrible. Horrible," he says.

I hear him wipe his nose, clear his throat.

"Oh my god, dad, what's going on? Are you alright? Is mom ok?" "We're fine," he says, shuddering out a little sob.

"What is it, dad?" I ask, frantic.

"It's the fish," he says. I slump in my chair. It's the fucking fish.

"Oh, no, dad, what happened?" I ask, trying to sound soothing, trying to sound like I care.

He gulps down a hiccup. "Water bugs, real bad. They came in droves, just started yesterday. Ate 'em," he says, devolving into further tears.

"What do you mean, ate 'em?" I ask.

"Ate 'em!" he says, loud. "Ate 'em right up, overnight, didn't stand a chance! Oh, it's horrible," he says, his words coming out in spurts between sobs. "You should've seen the pond, Tilly, I've never seen anything so terrible in my life. Red with blood and the fish just floating on top, huge chunks out of them. None of the eggs are gonna make it, choked out, water's more blood than anything," he says, trailing off.

I'm horrified. "Oh my god, dad, that's awful," I say, not knowing what else to say. "Your mother's been crying all day," he says, calming a bit. "We haven't lost a school like this since, gosh, since you were a kid, wasn't it? That one winter when the pond froze and it was too cold for us to go outside to check on 'em?"

I shiver at the memory. "Yeah," I say, "Oh, wow, Dad. I'm so sorry."

"Little Jimmy, Carla, Spots, Queenie," he says, and I can just see him shaking his head, "They were good fish."

"They were good fish," I say.

—————

The halls of the museum are long and tall, domed glass panels overhead letting in stark winter light. My footfalls echo and I feel self conscious of the sound. I stand in front of paintings for a long time to avoid having to move. I allow my eyes to wander. They land on a red button, a bit of dimpled flesh, little furrows of trees in the distance, a startled rabbit, a woman with her face turned toward a fire. Seeing is simple. My mind clears. A pear. A platter of pearls. A headless man and a woman wielding a bloody sword.

I round the corner out of the gallery and I'm startled to see Dario's name in huge letters across the opposite wall. Beneath his name, a black door. A guard ushers me in, finger to lips. The space within is pitch dark. I walk forward, hands out. I feel two walls on either side. I hear little breaths ahead in the distance, shuffling feet, and I walk toward the sounds. The passage is long and just when I start to feel frightened, a large screen emerges out of the black space, a shallow pool of light falling at its feet. I join the handful of people already there standing around the screen.

A close shot of two pairs of hands, one pair of hands caressing the other. The frame zooms out incrementally as the second pair of hands seems to resist the advances of the first. The first set of hands gets rough. The second set of hands is stiff, fearful. I'm losing interest, it's like a weird puppet show, when two things quickly happen at once. The first set of hands rips a finger off the other, tearing a long piece of skin all the way down the meat of the palm, I can almost feel it, and the frame zooms all the way out to reveal the bodies, the people to whom the hands belong. Dario and me.

I'm bewildered. It must be a dream.

I call Dario from the lobby of the museum, watching the snow swirl outside as it rings. Dario doesn't answer. I call him again, sure he's looking at his device, wherever he is. He answers on the last ring.

"Yes," he says, drawing out the word. I roll my eyes.

"You won't believe what I just saw," I say, trying to sound casual.

"Won't I?"

"Your installation. At the museum."

I hear him let out a frustrated scoff on the other end. "That old thing?"

"According to the giant poster in this lobby, it just opened last weekend. And it's up for another month. Why didn't you tell me?" I can hear myself getting worked up. I won't be out-charmed by him into thinking this is flattering.

He laughs. And ends the call.

Joseph Rathgeber

Capital Celebrates Its Orgies

We flirt with the idea of a threesome: deconstruct
the bedroom a bit. But where do you meet new
people nowadays? Not to be against Nature, though,

but who—*I ask you who*—is keeping track? These
studies show line graphs and declensions in all
items we hold sacred. Presidents' Day sales, for one;

Black Friday bonanzas with bullet brains, for another.
We will abolish gender for the hourly rate we pay
at the check-in counter of the King's Inn. Weekly

rates are available, and the rooms have Wi-Fi, HBO,
and two cup coffee makers. That will not do.
We have to do better. The employers want resiliency.

Boredom God

If you're not bored with poetry you ain't doing it
right. Vice is fucking the help. But it's going to
cramp like intestinal blockage on a Tuesday when

those fork tines tickle-stab your lower torso. In
and out, quicklike, like a cop gun popping off.
I'm bored to my heart's content: I just can't read

it anymore. I'm digging holes in dirt and biting my
nails afterwards, because the grit of it tastes better
than the beach-blowy pages of a crowdsourced

glossy lit magazine. Contributors' notes, though—
now there's a read. I run through them: a nimble
faerie with cellar dust flecked to my foot-bottoms.

You Thought It Was This, But It's That

"Wellness" and "mindfulness" are akin to
the alarm-orange Home Depot bucket in the corner
of the classroom:

full of sand, antibacterial soap, and water w/
                          expiration dates.

Active-shooting situations last an average of five
minutes,   studies say,   but the lockdown

                         can last
                         for hours
                         while you
                         wait for
                         cops

to clear each
corner of the building.   Some people
react to stress   by shitting;   others tighten
       their assholes.

[*squatting over a bucket   w/ your peers*
                  watching]

Meditating in class is like that. Cueing up a guided
meditation w/ flower petals unfolding
psychedelically through strobes and breathing
deliberately and lavender diffusing and artificial
light switched   off   and self-caring.

I don't need a bucket to shit in.

They don't need secular prayer.

I don't want to learn how to survive shooters and stress.

Stop   what   makes   living   so   hard.

Things need abolishing. / Then we can talk.

1967
From Earth

Shayla Lawz

we were all born in 1967
it was the year of keeping everything alive

you can call everything love

i often think about the life i could be living
just like a star

perhaps the love song is a call for us to stay
HERE, in this world
(perhaps love, too)

come back to earth

what was life like before it all happened?
that night we found the moon

i want to mail a postcard to my therapist to tell her that i'm fine
but all month i've been trying to find the post office
things get lost like that sometimes
and people do, too

you can be yourself here

you were knocking at the door
before i called you

everything is alive somewhere
if i knew where i'd tell you

i know we all want to believe that any of us
can survive alone

what did you love?

i am trying to forgive
i am learning about flight
the moments before & after

Andrew Gibeley

Emma Watson

Mom and Dad would yell *poop*
to make our Rottweiler poop
in the dead brush dividing
our land and the Foleys' and
the family's before the Foleys
I'll always be too young to remember
but I do remember the house
turning yellow to green in days
and the windows stark white

And she pooped as she was told.

Actually Emma was a Rottweiler mix
but with what we never really knew
a German Shepherd complexion,
hints of Pitbull in her build,
Chow Chow Mom presumed by
the blackened tongue spots that
flopped wet on summer nights in
suburbia where my friends and I
killed insects in the lamppost light
with electrified tennis rackets that
reminded Mom somehow of Auschwitz

And Emma ate some of their corpses.
Watson was the Foleys' Basset Hound

one year Emma's junior whom
they brought home second
after a toothy hound bit the daughter
I think is named Elena and
sent it back to the canine society
where I sometimes volunteered with
a non for profit called Kids 4 Paws
my friend Erika formed in service to
pet Katrina victims which Mom was
certain would get her into Harvard

But she only got into Middlebury.

We all called Watson Emma's boyfriend
though he basically just sniffed her
butthole and licked an inner ear or two
while she peed her dominance on his
lawn beyond the turd brush which
I'm sure I saw Elena playing in with
her brother I used to throw plastic balls
with on weekends up and down the
rooftop of our two-car garage

But I've sniffed non-boyfriends' butts too.

Emma and Watson hooked up
twelve years until she got cancer in
her bones the fall I turned twenty
and died one day in January when
I was studying in Scotland so
Mom and Dad Skyped me the news
and I spent the night sobbing in

my dorm room while my friends
went out clubbing with table service
vodka cranberry and soda refills

And Watson died one year after that.

I Build Lots Of Sandcastles

instead of one great tall one
in front of me forever like a mirror
or that capital b best friend
I worry others see me as
more often than I see them as mine,
though I suppose neither of us
will ever really know for sure

Then I worry that makes me
seem selfish or just feel
stuck-up for thinking so,
elevating my perceived worth
to a humanitarian extrovert,
offering up my love and
companionship like a service
like a coffeeshop fringe ad
to pluck and put in your pocket,
and then I feel charitable
and thereby pleased
like when my future wife died
before me on the cardboard
life map I made in middle school
so the poor thing would
never have to live without me

Is it enough being doubtfully
loved by so many when
I spend days questioning
my true love for many more?
Is some part of all this

simply affecting others,
stretching my smile as far
and as wide as it can stretch,
instead of owning up to those
raw, rare emotional truths
that keep me second guessing,
blowing smoke into shadows
off my sixth floor fire escape,
watching my butterfly wings
float away with the wind?

What Are U Looking For

you ask me, DM me
phone dings and there's your nipple
white, hairy, wrinkled around the edges
you're balding on top and I picture Poppop
Dates Fun and Stuff you call yourself
68 years old—you are bear, jock,
Daddy, you typed
I'm high and reading memoir

Sunday scaries creep the room
Yankee candle burning, twilight looms
my roommate's away
and I almost consider it,
imagine your muffin tops
envision varicose veins
the thinning hair in your ears
small moles and skin tags

Another ding and there it is
curved like a croissant
color of an eraser
a pleather cock ring seeming
to shorten it—
Hey sexy I type you back
a childlike reflex, the Golden rule
regretting actively in real time

I can see it enter me
and smell your old, wet lube
can feel the hollow and the raw

and wonder if you take Cialis,
then I see Poppop's prescriptions
their plastic tubes, abstruse labels
every day of the week initialed
boldly on their little squares

Another ding and I turn the fucking sound off
my right index finger shaking
red oval marks the spot
a brownstone I presume, rent-controlled
two miles separate thrill and remorse
but out my window I see only bricks
and expanding darkness, so I gather
my bearings in my empty full bed
and I call Poppop

Quietus

The night before we unplugged you
we ate burritos and accidentally entered
a Petco before buying a large white
poster board to collage your life's photos
upon for everyone to enjoy at the
post-funeral luncheon on Friday

We visited you one last morning
and there were air-pumped plastic sheets
like pool rafts along your hairless legs
which I pressed down with my fingers
so your frail, pale skin was unexposed
to the elements of the ICU, which smelled
raw and stale and sounded silent

The nurse told us it could take hours
or even a day or two since you still
breathed on your own a bit over the
ventilator tubed down your throat
but you died within minutes before all
our crying eyes, choking viciously
on your final gasps of air, then nothing

That night the summer sky erupted
thunder storming all around us while we
drove through the dark in the downpour
to pick up our 9:30 pizza and white wine
as your umbrella broke in my hands
and your body sat idle in the morgue
waiting out the lightning like us

The Surrender of Man

Naomi Falk

"Bury me deep enough that the earth / will push me into something new."

> —Chuks Ndulue, "Sacrifices at the Altar of the Chicken"

Through the ashes I bend. Every time I've tried to close my eyes to be consumed by blackness, out of nothing the words begin. This lonely river is ceaseless. Sometimes I cannot sleep, I catch myself talking to myself, casting thoughts to nowhere. Not sure of the meaning of what is being said, but there is a heartbeat, an unchanging tone to the words. It is a low tone—long serpentine ultraviolet waves. What I hear is deeper than the frequency of my voice, and I wonder if I produce it or if it comes to me uncontrollably. The words move with convicted velocity toward an unrecognizable dimension. My tongue tenses and curls in shape of the words, saying the words inside the cave of my mouth. I know not when they commence but I am purposeful in trying to end them so as not to be controlled by them.

The words stalk my thoughts as I cross my ankles on the subway or wash my face with a bar of soap. It is only in purposefully listening to the words that I realize they course through my mind; my attention to them interrupts them. But as they grow acquainted to being noticed, the words resume their usual incantatory rhythm. The menial tasks of which my life is composed become but a backdrop for the words— too many words—passing through this mind. If the words hope to entrench me, I'll unearth myself through exposing them.

And now, as I'm writing the words they become less clear than they were before they left my head. By the light of day they grow garish. To which of my senses do the words belong? As they are realized in my mind, tumbling from primal sound into signifier, they stretch into eleventh-dimensional shapes. The words can't stay, even as I write them here. Trying to recall them after witnessing them is a practice in memorization, not a practice in creation. I'm just reciting.

Even in the deepest hours of twilight, as the world envelops its contents in the palette of slumber, the words whisper to me. They tell me that my dreams—when I used to dream—were a meaningless distraction from consciousness. What used to be sleep is now an archangel of overwhelming restlessness, hours of lying at the mercy of the words. They keep me awake boundlessly through the night and into morning. Now how to live? When the sun crosses the horizon's threshold, I feel myself exposed. My pupils retract because they are disgusted by the arrival of another day, and I cower below the sheets in pursuit of a sleep that will not come. All I can do is lust for rest, craft a blanket of nostalgia for a time when it was silent.

In the hours of the afternoon, I am moving through a world in which I once flourished, talking with beings and forms I knew in a past life, now guided by the words. On the street, the sound of my companion's voice loses its apexes and valleys, becoming some language I no longer understand spoken in slow and monochromatic syllables. I'm not sure what it is I'm supposed to be hearing. The outlines of her face and the rigid telephone pole behind her bleed into the gutter, stretching into indistinct oblong shapes pulled downward by a new, heavier gravity.

I know that it is the words distorting my senses, but I no longer perceive anything recognizably comforting. What's the point? I wander off alone. I consume myself with the passing of time / by looking at the clock, daunting of the universe at the stroke of midnight. Is this forever now? I know that I am dying; I only wish it to come quicker.

I gaze at my feet when I no longer care enough to hold my head up. It looks as though I can see through the ground. Down below and much to my chagrin, all the versions of myself to've walked this earth labor in the circles. This isn't hell; it's a reflection that allows me to see inside myself. I am eternally damned; decaying from the inside out. In this mirror, roaches gnaw at my heels and chatter on my shoulders, glistening in the reflection of the sweat burning canyons into my neck. The words want me to pay for the moments of my life in which I failed to produce the desired result. Punished for this terrible posture, the tendencies I could not control, for the woman I've been: those were the times I separated from myself, acting out of a desire for liberation from my own constraints. I never thought I would die hating myself. My questions about death were so paltry and focused on whether or not I'd achieved anything great. I never thought to take my temperature along the way. Had I known then what I'd feel now, I question if I'd have trodden more carefully, with calculation. The words grow louder and swell within me, choking me until I can no longer breathe. They hold me at the edge of asphyxiation.

In a final act of defiance, I close my eyes and imagine a way out of my subservience to the words. What I see around me and inside myself is now terrifying. The darkness I cherished during my life has lost its seduction. There are no oceans to cross, so where do I come ashore? The beauty of our world is eradicated by me as I am now beholden to the words. I cannot ignore what they have shown me about me.

There is nothing to do but try to live my life as I had before the words began, performing the acts that had foundationalized my being for all those years. But now, when I reach out to feel the sky or to caress the silver chain around my lover's neck, the words absorb the colors. Cerulean and metal, the phenomena of our world, snake toward my claws and into my veins, dulling the vibrancy of my surroundings until all dims to a bordeaux so deep it blinds me. The words force me to retreat inside myself, and, from my womb, I finally suffocate on the blood that once sustained me, the life that was given to me in hopes that I would become a life of my own. But I no longer perceive the space in which I move.

The words have unraveled me, everything I loved. I am that which I fear, destroyer of all I touch. The acreage of my flesh is condemned: it's doomsday now.

■

Those visions of myself toiling below were but illusions, perhaps put in place because the words knew I thought it was what I deserved. I was seduced by what would have been a fantastical end.

There is nothing here in limbo but memory. I wrap my arms around my knees. The fact, I notice momentarily, is that I am not physically existing at all. I am just the projection of a sense, able to see without being seen. Of course, I can't know for sure, but I surmise it. I'd felt looked down upon so often during my life, as I suppose everyone did in the privacy of her thoughts. I could never discern what role I was meant to play. That anxiety has dissolved now, and nothing but the space around me fills the space around me. It's not that I'm weight-less—a force presses upon me. It is the force of all that to which I've borne witness and all that in which I've partaken. It cradles my car-cassless being, peers down into my hazy presence. I cannot remember my life without it regarding me, too. The memories crowd together, though. Unholy matrimony between ourselves and what haunts us...

My rainboots sink into the grass in a field full of bees, so full that I refuse to walk but instead cry until my mother picks me up, and the grey morning light slanting through my window is so bright that I know he has left me forever. When I learned that he ate his wife's ashes in his cereal every day after she had been cremated, I built a memorial for myself in the forest, a place to bury—like Mathews said—the leaves at the bottom of a well. The walls were too low. I saw the man lift the cigarette to his mouth and tumble backward over the ledge. This occurred in the quiet hour of the night, I gasped for breath and peered below to witness his body stretched on the pavement between the house and the parking lot. But, in a moment of distraction, the raven that landed on the banister was smoking a Marlboro red, like a cowboy. The dark lord of my dreams! Through corridors of Persian rugs I desperately searched for help, or even just an answer. The one door that opened revealed a scene in which his mother held a shotgun to his dog's head. I subsumed the pain of another that would last the rest of my life, and, upon my arrival at the mouth of the cave during avalanche season, I forgot the rest of the song. What key was it in, even? I continued pressing into the keys, quite arbitrarily, unsurprised to hear him telling me he'd be gone by la primavera. His eyes saw mine as the ocean—so undividedly— in the neon smoke of the room that I started to cry. I didn't mind the twisters forming on the horizon, because it never seemed they'd come near enough to destroy me. The few times I'd felt proximity, I'd inexplicably arrived at the eye of the storm. He didn't remember telling me that he loved me, and neither do I remember being loved. I declined an invitation to the funeral, and got on the ship to cross the ocean before recalling I'd been booked a flight. I whispered to myself that the pain would pass as a dewy petal returning to the earth in the shadow of a break in the trees. How is it that women never die?

How is it that we pluck these moments from our histories, retroactively and without knowing why? It could be that they stayed with me all along. How to know what is important enough to keep? It wasn't clear to me then and it wouldn't be clear until years later, even after I had finished considering it, even now, as I consider it. I guess time and age distilled what was important.

Although sorrow shines brightly over our memories, it comes from somewhere unreachable, like a glittering orb lodged in the sand of the chilly ocean floor. A sleepwalk drifted below every waking and unconscious act of my years—a part of my life formed outside of my control. It began quietly until it gained enough strength to voice itself, and thus began the words. They were born of regret, of longing, of self-loathing. I mistook my blue feelings as a side effect of human life, when it was most often that case that I allowed sadness to overtake me without a fight. It grew within before radiating.

Perhaps in my lifetime, the experience of womanhood was inextricable from an overwhelming sense of guilt. The experience of girlhood was buffered by the pressure to obsessively self-reflect. I berated my own actions, believing I was poisonous. The responsibility was too great. I was torn between self-victimization and self-loathing, and leaning too hard toward either led me to fall into the other.

I had always survived off reading, because it unburdened me of the emotions in which I ensnared myself. There was one thing I did not realize until now, until after my own death. The narratives of our world, regardless of the color of emotion or the breadth of intellect, all revealed how poorly we understand our role in the lives of others.

The course of my own life taught me one thing: that I was owed love by no one.

The appendages of memory untangle and separate upon my confrontation of them, until they hover about me like stillborn snakes. Past them is nothing but space, field of unvaried carnelian. When my blood was spilled by the words it replaced the air around me and began to expand unflinchingly.

I never would have apprehended *this* continuation of myself before my own eyes in the afterlife. I was told, and believed, that death was a sleep robed in crimson and gold. I was an atheist before I had the language to express it, but I had always been enraptured by the other people's ideas about belief, in their conviction that a higher power configured into the chaos and order of their lives. So much of my life had been spent wondering what it would be like to have this dependency, this certainty in being held accountable for your actions and knowing the price you must pay for them.

One memory: I am fidgeting in the pew on Sunday morning, looking through the pages of the bible, and I always loved how fragile they were. Almost translucent. I behold the language on the pages with joy; I dip in and out of understanding the contents. Such musicality and tonality. That year, my fourth-grade teacher had asked me why I wanted to do a book report on Charles Dickens, and I told her it reminded me of the King James Bible.

The pastor has finally arrived at the end of the sermon. I hadn't been listening, having always found him and his unadorned Lutheran pulpit underwhelming. Behind him, a huge window exposes the field behind the church, so that is another thing I do as I wait for this to be over. I look out. After filing out of the pews, old women stand in rows on either side of the double-doors, handing us palm fronds. I am small and the palms arch over me, and I am in the forest. I carry my frond toward the red exit sign, surprised at the slightness of its stem, tender like a mouse's ribcage. I want to protect it. When I emerge from the tunnel, the lobby is filled with noon light, and the room, which is usually flat and sallow, is luminescent—as if reflecting moving water—against people dressed so finely. My mother hands me her palm frond, and now I have two. I fan them above my head, squinting to see the way they move. That I'd been neither baptized nor crowned by any religion crossed my mind; it often did when I was here. Today seemed like it would have been the right day for it—a baptism—in this golden light, dipped back into untroubled water, in this golden light, a birth in the afternoon.

The most beautiful images of childhood are fraught with longing, because you think that earlier versions of yourself, more ignorant versions, were unburdened by the years to come.

———

A faint bell rings from far away, and the strands of memory dissipate. My past becomes enigmatic to me, and I am returned bent into a knotted clutch. I untangle my limbs and release my fingers from my palms to find I've carried nothing into the final stage of death.

My life was only something I caught whispers of in passing, like a sad story. I am conflicted in knowing I'm now alone with this mysterious loss. Deep inside, an impenetrable scab has formed. I look for it, finding the gilt entrance to a tomb. When I lean against the door, I hear a faint twinkle, like the sound one thinks of upon seeing the gleam of one million platinum bars under a spotlight in an otherwise dark room. I retract in horror, but the little sound stays. A part of me has been taken away.

Phil Anderson

Campus Tour, Part 1
Jacob Woods, 2002

I. The French Building

Finn Hardy came to Woods's office to ask for a letter of recommendation. He squeezed his bulky body into the small, carved-wood chair that, while old, was still only half the age of the school that had bought it.

"I'll be applying to colleges that have emphasises—"

"Emphases."

"Emphases, yeah, duh. Emphases on creative writing."

"Oh?"

"I want to," he said, "be a poet. Like you. I think."

Finn had never taken a class with Woods, and the teacher told him that it was highly irregular for him to write a letter of recommendation for a student he hasn't taught. Finn turned around and looked at the office door, ajar, as he considered his next words.

"I just figured," the boy said, and it became Woods's turn to look past the doorframe to the dark hallway. As an English teacher, Jacob Woods, MFA, was quartered in the basement of the French building—so named for the obscure eighteenth-century American poet and one-time instructor of Literature at the Credence Academy, Reginald Quincy French. (French, the language, was taught in the Lyman Latin Library.) Finn had come for this impromptu meeting during Woods's conference hours in his Thursday free period. The office was not solely his, but one he shared with Dr. Carson who was presently starting her AP class. In the silence that fell after *figured*, they heard the footfalls of tardy students stammer above them. There were the snapping closed of doors and a few requisite guffaws as teachers tried to quell the autumnal giddiness of students who had found their scholastic groove and had already given up worries of academic success for the anxieties of impressing their classmates. The basement office had poor natural light that stuttered in, between the shadows of shifting clouds and swaying trees and moving legs, through the three-foot wide window that started at the ceiling and extended down a foot to where the ground outside lay.

Woods walked over to the door and closed it. It was an especially gray day—as all are in Maine in October—so he lit a desk lamp before returning to his chair.

"Finn," he began. "Of course I'll write you a letter of recommendation."

The boy smiled and dropped deeper into the creaking chair, a move that sunk his square head into his thick neck and caused his legs to bow out.

"But understand," he dropped his voice, "that I will be writing it from the position of how well, ostensibly, we know each other."

"Ostensibly?"

"That is," he said, "for example, freshman year: 'He was one of ten or eleven students that had been assigned to me for a few hours during Unity Days. We went around the circle, said our names, our favorite foods, where we're from and what we did last summer.'"

"Finn Hardy, lasagna, Washington DC—"

"'That summer he had gone to Italy. He had appreciated the Sistine Chapel. After introductions, I had the students write an exquisite-corpse poem,'" despite Dr. Carson suggesting Woods have them make acrostics of their names; it was his first year teaching, and she had deigned to be his mentor. Still, these were young adults, not kindergarteners.

"'It was then that I first saw Mr. Hardy's keen interest in poetry,' blah blah blah, 'but our time together ended when Mr. Gordon came to take the group to do a ropes course and trust falls.'"

"Right."

Woods told Finn he could discuss their regular conversations in his capacity as Weekend Events Manager, a glorified name for weekend van chauffeur. All teachers were required some extracurricular duties, and since he was never a theater person and couldn't coach a sport, Woods was assigned to drive a school van once a weekend for off-campus trips. He took students to malls or movie theaters or to downtown Portland or Portsmouth so the boarders whose parents lived farther than a few hours out could have some semblance of teenage life beyond the confines of Credence Academy's heavily wooded, insular campus. Starting his sophomore year, Finn was in the van whenever his sporting schedule allowed (freshmen were not allowed the luxury of leaving campus). The boy often sat shotgun because at fifteen he was already six-foot-two and liked to stretch out. For those hour-long car rides the two would politely talk about the weather, the seasons, and the increase of Support Our Troops stickers as they passed the state line into New Hampshire.

"Though of course," Woods said, "I suppose I could say that *that* was when we talked about the New York School and the Beats and the tepid blandness of having Billy Collins as our poet laureate."

"Here." Finn sat up, and from his chinos pulled two pieces of computer paper folded eight times. "One is a list of the schools, the other is a recent poem."

He placed the papers on the desk and stood.

"Be sure to still ask your dorm parents and coaches to write letters," Woods said.

Finn came around behind the desk, and the teacher eyed the closed door. In the classroom above them, twelve students sat around a Harkness table, Dr. Carson at the head, and she led them in conversation around, probably, the social pressures that stifle the affections of Newland Archer in *The Age of Innocence*. The general theme of this year's English curriculum was simply: Love, American Style. Stanley, the Department Head, proffered that turd at the June meeting. "A response to the American war effort in Iraq. If there'll be War abroad, let's have some Love at Credence." Finn ignored Woods's darting eyes and kissed him on the forehead.

"Of course I will still be asking my dorm parents and coaches to write letters, Woods," the boy whispered at the teacher's temple. "But at least I'll get to read yours before it goes out, won't I?"

The boy left, and left the door open.

Woods unfolded the two pieces of paper on the desk. He noticed the list had a mix of small liberal arts colleges and some D-1 football schools. The boy was clearly undecided of his future. The poem was free-verse and titled "Augustine Reads Luke":

> *Woman loses drachma, uses lamp*
> *She'll light the patterns on the rug*
> *Lamp-light the corners of gray matter*
> *What when the woman loses memory*
> *Of losing the drachma in the gray*
> *What when the woman lamps the rug*
> *And the pattern matches memory*
> *And a drachma found remembered*
> *What when finding memory is lost*
> *Woman loses drachma, uses lamp*

Woods read it through a few times, unconsciously counting syllables and testing the meter, observing the use of assonance and consonance and off-rhymes, like *matter* and *pattern*, and the sheer repetition of words. Why *drachma*? he wondered. Though he found the music of the word interesting, especially its consonant order, an affricate and liquid to a velar stop to the bilabial nasal; *drachma* is practically the Carrollian "Drink me." But as it stood, the poem was nonsense. Woods wondered if Finn shouldn't try to turn this draft into a villanelle or sestina, stretch his idea out but keep the structure limited. Better to learn and master the fixed verses before one moves onto free verse, his cohort had been admonished in graduate school: "Picasso could draw a photorealist bull, so you have to write a perfect limerick." The entire first semester workshop at the MFA was sonnets and quatrains and double dactyls. Woods underlined every instance of the word *memory* on Finn's poem and wrote "dactyl." The hallway remained untrod for the entire period.

He placed the papers in a bottom file drawer for which he alone had a key, then went upstairs for his senior elective class, War Novels. He had pitched the class that summer to Stanley, a response to his response. The department head okayed it with the caveat that Woods didn't use the class to repudiate the President. "We're a hop, skip, and a nature hike away from Kennebunkport," he had told him. "Plus I'm sure there's at least one kid at Credence whose dad is in the adminis-tration. Hardy, right?"

"The class will be about rounding out an understanding of the artistic value of war," Woods had told him, not very sure of what he said. But Stanley liked to hear things had artistic value, and the old man suggested *For Whom the Bell Tolls* or *A Farewell to Arms* for the syllabus. Woods decided they were both too long, so instead he agreed to assign *The Sun Also Rises* to appease Stanley's Hemingway fetish (Stanley himself had a big beard and a penchant for fisher-man turtlenecks—he would blend well into the background of the Portland docks).

The coursework of War Novels attracted mostly male students. The louder ones were hawkish, and spent the hour picking apart Tim O'Brien's narrator as weak-willed, or "a prime example of why there shouldn't be any homos in the Army."

"What about the Navy?" Woods asked, earnestly thinking of

a youthful tryst he had one summer in San Diego, but the students just laughed. Another called out, "Or Coast Guard!" The teacher had succeeded in locker room talk, even if by accident. He was, admittedly, not invested in the discussion, his mind oft returning to Finn and the innocent kiss from that morning. The risk of it, and the likely brunt of the punishment would be doled out to the teacher. Finn had just turned eighteen, but if anyone had seen a kiss as intimately boring as that, who could believe their affair had just begun that day? Woods looked around the classroom; there were only two girls in the class. One laughed with the boys, and the other shifted in her seat and stared at her copy of *The Things They Carried* on the large, oval table. He wanted to tell her he was sorry. Next week they were to read Marguerite Duras. He was sure that would exonerate him.

II. The Winthrop Building

After class Woods walked through the back parking lot of the Winthrop building to the rear entrance of the administration offices because he had his first ever meeting of the disciplinary committee. Every year the committee changes hands, and three faculty and three students are chosen by Dean Hasslebach and her assistant to assess accusations of plagiarism or drinking or sexual misconduct or whatever. Woods's Toyota was parked in this parking lot, and, passing it, the teacher remembered his initial sexual misconduct with young Finn.

It had been the first Saturday of Spring break of the year before. The sign-up sheet for the van to Portsmouth had just one name on it. All the local students had been picked up by parents that morning or the night before, and the longer-distance boarders were sharing livery services to Logan. When Woods saw Finn's name scrawled on the clipboard that hung perennially outside the Dean of Student's office, he assumed there had been some mistake of dates. Still, he waited, and at the allotted hour the young mountain showed up in the front hall in a beanie, warm-up jacket and athletic shorts, despite the low temperature. He asked who else was coming. "Just me and you," Woods said, and Finn had smiled a smile the teacher recognized but couldn't then place. It was something eager, like Christmas morning.

They went to Portsmouth. Woods left the van on campus; instead they took his 4Runner. "Why are you still around?" Woods asked. Finn said he wanted to buy something specific before he left, and that he had to go New Hampshire to get it. "Plus, tax free," he said. "It's New Hampshire's only redeeming quality."

They parked in the main square, and Finn asked, with that same smile, if Woods wanted to come with him. On an average trip the teacher would disappear to a coffee shop, journal in hand, and pretend to write for a few hours while these kids, out of his sights, committed their various misdemeanors or capitalist endeavors. He would have waved Finn on, but he was curious about that smile. It trembled with nervousness, and he could sense how tense his body got as he made it. In retrospect, it was a gay bar smile—seeking, flirty, but scared to death. Woods hadn't stepped foot in a gay bar since shortly after graduate school; he was weary of the hunt and bored of the drugs, and he had grown out of laughing at the daddies doing poppers on the dance floor and grown into someone who found pleasure in staying in. He had a few failed dates in the intervening summers, and only once in the past four years had he broken his Mainely celibacy, at a writer's conference, with an ex from undergrad. It was dubious Finn would act on that smile, and Woods was sure he would put a stop to anything if the boy made a move, but he couldn't resist feeling wanted. So he followed Finn.

They went to a bookshop, his first surprise. The second surprise came when this big kid walked straight to the information desk and asked for a book he had put on order. The old biddy behind the counter took her time to sort through a stack of books rubber banded with paper slips. Finn's excitement was palpable, if not frantic. The woman returned to the counter and handed Finn a slim volume of poetry: *Drake Equations for the None I Love*. By Jacob Woods. Finn had special ordered his book.

They got coffee in the bookstore cafe because Finn wanted to discuss Woods's poetry, and poetry in general. Woods asked who Finn's favorite poets were, and the boy said Walt Whitman, Allen Ginsberg, Hart Crane. There was a pattern of lifestyle if not verse style, and the teacher prodded further, asking him what it was about these poets he liked so much, why them? Finn shrugged, then said, "They all had a lot of passion, and they have three different styles in expressing that passion." He added, "Whitman wanted to be everybody, Ginsberg wanted to be himself, and Crane didn't want anything but to play with language."

"Crane wanted sailors," Woods said. "Or he wanted sailors to love him."

Finn muttered something into his coffee mug, then he looked up and asked Woods, "Why is your book called *Drake Equations for the None I Love*?"

Woods had done a limited reading tour of a few cities after the book came out—independent bookstores New York, Philadelphia, Boston, D.C. Each place had asked him about the title and the Drake equation, and he always told a grand lie about a true love, a physicist, who died in a Duck Boat accident in the Charles River. But today he felt compelled to truth.

"Do you know what the Drake equation is?"

The boy didn't.

"Me either, really. I'm a charlatan at best, Finn. I glean all my ideas from things overheard, from lectures I go to where I forget to take notes, and from smarter people I've had the chance to have a few dinners with before we disappear from each other's lives."

The boy stared at Woods's hands as they fidgeted with his coffee cup.

"The Drake equation is what astronomers or whoever use to come up with the possibility of intelligent life on other planets. It breaks the thought down into fractions. So we start with the amount of stars in the galaxy, and then we winnow it down to the amount of stars that have planets, then we look at the planets that have certain elements that can support life, but then you also have to factor in time—remember we didn't always have intelligent life on our planet, and we probably won't for much longer. All this is to say that the chance of aliens coming to talk to us are so miniscule because of the all the variables that are in the Drake equation. Again, I'm a charlatan, so I don't know how to better explain it. I dated someone who went to MIT." Woods looked into his empty coffee mug. "Finn, you know I'm gay, right?"

"I mean, all the students assumed."

"Well the someone I dated from MIT was a guy who told me about the Drake equation, and I said it was like being gay, wasn't it? He said, 'How do you mean?' And I recounted that statistically ten percent of the U.S. population is homosexual, and even then that statistic more likely includes everyone in the queer LGBT umbrella, so let's say there's only four percent of gay men, then factor in how many of them are out, then factor in the age of these men, factor in the places where they live, whether or not they'd have the right interests, the right chemistry. I told him that falling in love while being gay is about as dire as finding intelligent life in our galaxy."

"Sounds like there's still a chance, which negates your title. There could be a one instead of a none, even if the odds are against it."

"Not for me, I don't think. But don't let my pessimism discourage you if you are—"

"I'm not."

"Well," Woods said. "I hope you like the book."

"Whatever happened to the MIT guy?"

"How do you mean?"

"What did he think of your Drake equation?"

"He realized I wasn't his intelligent life but he assumed there was one for him out there." Woods stood. "We should get a move on."

In the car ride back to campus, at a red light, Finn placed his oversize fist on Woods's thigh and leaned his head to his ear to say something, except no words came out. He pulled his hand away as compulsively as he placed it, and Woods pulled into a Stop-n-Shop parking lot and parked far off from the other cars. Finn looked near the verge of tears, and when Woods reached for his shoulder to calm him, Finn grabbed the teacher's shirt collar and pulled his face to his.

The kiss went on, and Woods kept expecting to stop it, to pull away, but he never did. Soon the teacher saw the boy's erection tent his shorts, and after a few unspoken glances, Woods's hand was rubbing the crotch above the mesh. He pulled away, quickly, with a realizing sensation of serious trespass.

"Why are you stopping," Finn protested.

The teacher said this was inappropriate, had gone too far. "I'm sorry," he said, and he felt a sickly mixture of fear, shame and lust, something he felt in small amounts consistently over the years. It was the same feeling he had as a pubescent boy when his friend caught the young Jake Woods looking at him in their Catholic high school locker room. His friend's eyes sparked fear and hatred as he noticed Woods staring at his pubic hair that trailed down from his stomach, and at his uncircumcised penis—Woods was fascinated by the hood that covered its head. He had never seen anything like it before, and his mind froze in wonderment, his mouth agape. He was caught. That boy sensed lust and covered himself, walked away. It was not long before he had tacitly ended their friendship—and all Woods's social allyships, really—by telling everyone in school that Jake Woods was "some kind of faggot."

He remembered that phrasing as Finn sat hunched over in passenger seat staring at the dashboard, or his life beyond it. He remembered "some kind of faggot" because at fourteen years old he thought it was stupidly vague, as if there were varieties of faggotry, as if he weren't just the one kind. But now he realized that desires were various and with differing degrees of acceptance. He wanted Finn just now as he had wanted that friend—to use a Catholic word, covetously—and it was a desire Woods had not admitted to himself or understood, a desire he repressed deeper than his sexuality because homosexuals were on a path to acceptance, and pederasty was ancient and Hellenistic and out of vogue, no longer a part of the culture, mainstream or queer. And besides, wasn't he trying to avoid the culture? Is that not why Woods was living remotely in Maine on a rural high school campus many miles from an urban center with a queer community and vital gay bar scene? He had wanted to build a purity of mind that could reflect in his poetry, to write not of men and unrequited love and its miseries like Crane or Robert Duncan. He wanted to write aesthetics, to consider the functions and beauty of objects. Woods wanted to write pastorals like Frost; he did not want to, like Ginsberg, follow the ghost of a touchy Walt Whitman around a California supermarket as he lurks at the shop boys, but here he was sitting in a Stop-n-Shop parking lot with a young man looking like a Marsden Hartley subject with his dick tumescent in his beat up truck.

"This is all I've wanted, for months now," Finn broke the silence. And he lunged for Woods. He forced his tongue in the teacher's mouth and gripped his nape, pulling him down and toward him. Woods found he could not fight it, not because the boy's strength—and Finn was strong—but because his own weakness. His face was at the boy's crotch, finishing what he had started. *Who killed the pork chops? What price bananas?* he had thought. *Are you my angel?*

The disciplinary committee meeting was brief. It was a round of introductions: the teachers were Woods; Mrs. Kinney, the chemistry marm; and Mr. Gordon, a math teacher and, more importantly, the football coach. The students were of the typical sickly goody two-shoes types: Ginny Carson, Dr. Carson's overachiever daughter; Tyler Williams, an effeminate boy with a type-A personality; and Christine Park, selected probably to represent the population of Korean students who every year get caught smoking cigarettes just outside campus borders. Dean Hasslebach, a woman with a shock of white hair and a shockingly tanned and wrinkled face in a permanent turtleneck (she, too, looked as though she would fit in at the Portland docks), gave the new disciplinary committee a rundown of the various charges that have come up in the past and the typical punishments the charges accrue.

"You'll see over the course of the scholastic year both minor and major offenses as is routine every single year. We keep the deliberations of this committee strictly confidential in order to best protect the dignity of our students and the Credence legacy, but we cannot sweep all things under the rugs. Plagiarism, for example, is grounds for expulsion on first offense. As are anything deemed by the state of Maine to be felonious, such as distribution of controlled substances or certain assaults—"

Tyler Williams' hand shot up. He spoke when the dean raised an inquisitive eyebrow. "Will a student know how we voted in regards to their punishment?"

"That is confidential, as well," Hasslebach said.

"What if a teacher commits a felony?" Ginny chimed in. "Like what if Mr. Woods here starting selling ecstasy to freshman?"

"Virginia," Dean Hasslebach sighed. "It is wholly inappropriate to accuse Mr. Woods, even in jest… I'm sorry, Jacob."

"Sorry, Jake," Ginny whispered. She elbowed his arm, winked.

Hasslebach distributed red binders with student duties to Ginny, Tyler, and Christine, then dismissed the group. She asked Woods to lag behind. Kinney and Gordon each glanced back, curious, and

Gordon seemed almost to laugh as he left.

"These are the typical punishments," she said after all were gone, "but I want you know, as this is your first time on this committee, that there are other factors we must take into consideration when it comes to the discipline we dole out. That is, what the student contributes to the community, especially in the matters of diversity and extracurriculars and so on and so forth. What are their contributions."

"Contributions?" Woods asked, and just as happened in class earlier that day, his earnest question was mistaken for some chummy subtext. Hasslebach smiled, shrugged her broad shoulders and nudged him out the door, and she only said, "Well yes," before walking away.

Photo by Brendan Burdzinski

Photo by Brendan Burdzinski

The Sages on the Mountains, Acrylic on canvas, 79 x 60 inches, 2019 by Chunbum Park (early draft)

The Sages on the Mountains, Acrylic on canvas, 79 x 60 inches, 2019 by Chunbum Park

From *ceallaigh at kilmainham* by Kelly Gallagher (2013)

From *ceallaigh at kilmainham* by Kelly Gallagher (2013)

Andrea Stella

The rain rockets down into the street. It's louder than the music playing in this burlesque show at Hotel Chantelle. Austin and I are underdressed in tank tops and soggy shoes. We sneak out halfway through the set. July night steam hovers over the sidewalk as we stroll north from Essex to Avenue A with my freshly shaven head.

This chick stops us at the corner of St. Mark's asking for directions. She just got to the city from San Francisco with a bike and a chef's knife bag strapped to the handlebars. She shoves her hand across the back of my shaved head and tells Austin *his girlfriend is hot.*

He's not my boyfriend.

We walk to International on 1st and drink Bud Lights. She's worried about her bike, and I want to smoke a cigarette, so we stand outside on the curb, leaving the beers on the counter.

She gets close and kisses Austin. Austin pulls away and kisses me. I stand still getting kissed by her with his lips. We leave.

Austin brings us back to his roof on 11th and 1st. We strip down and lay on the warm tar. She spreads my legs with her teeth. Austin tries to get off next to us, but can't.

I leave my body and bounce up into the stars. As I watch from above, she fucks me harder than he ever could.

I come back down and they've both fallen asleep naked, one curled up on either side of me. I am satisfied, bruised, and numb. The summer sky is black and wide.

The day of the funeral Uncle Pete pulls me aside while we're walking up the hill of the cemetery to bury the urn.

- Stop by Aunt Ellen's before you go back to the city.

Uncle Joe has been cooking sausage and peppers, the kitchen air is thick and nostalgic. Uncle Pete hands me a little container.

- I hope you're not upset, but I separated Daddy. I'm taking some back to Florida and you girls can have this if you want it.

I ride home with Dad in my lap. I paid for the funeral, so why not get this as a party bag.

Sometimes I take him out and talk to him. Sometimes I use him as a party trick when we have people over if I've had too much wine

Want to see my dad?

Dad's in a plastic baggie inside of a small round Ziplock container with a neon green clear lid. He stays in my closet with my shirts. I make sure Dad's never in a room where I will have sex.

Draft Dodgers (Excerpt)

Etan Nechin

Inorodtsy

My great-great-great-grandfather was a thief of names. No one knows for sure, but he might have stolen four or five names throughout his brief life.

We only know his assumed name, the one he passed down illicitly to his son, all the way down to me. Some last names are more than an indication of genealogy, more than simply stating one is a scion of such and such; they're more than a moniker of a defunct occupation. In a few syllables, last names can shape the lives of those who bear them; they reverberate through centuries and geography and, like the cover of a book, they bind together many characters, lives, and ideas into a single story.

According to our family's story, my great-great-great-grandfather's birth name was Rabinovich. My grandfather, Marvelous Maximus, swore to it. He never said it directly to me, but my father swears he told him, and that it is, in fact, Rabinovich. My father said his father, Marvelous Maximus, knew this because once, when Marvelous Maximus was sixteen or seventeen, an old woman in a flowery shirt walked up to him when he was smoking cigarettes with his high school friends. She began patting his cheek, speaking in Russian. Marvelous Maximus didn't understand Russian, but he did remember she kept asking, "Rabinovich?" *Rabinovich?*

When Marvelous Maximus told his father about that incident, his father said that it might be true; there were Rabinoviches who had wood shops back in Rostov-on-Don, or so that's what his father told him.

This so-called Rabinovich wasn't a criminal—or, technically, he was—but like most thieves, he stole out of need. The names he stole were like bread; he stole to move forward, to survive.

His first crime was that he was poor. Not that he chose to be—poverty can be like a genetic disease. It determines a person's future, it's debilitating, and, most times, it's deadly. A cure is seldom found because poor people are usually quarantined with other poor people; in some societies, the punishment of poverty is met by those in power who believe it is justified because *those people—whoever they are— deserve to live in the lean, to have an existence of squalor and* short-age, their lives a constant crisis of want and hunger and illness and illiteracy. Degradation is never beyond the pale; it is the margin in which they exist. They're destined to remain nameless, subject to the whims of whoever is sitting on the seat of power, which in the case of the so-called Rabinovich, when he was in his mid-teens, the seat saw a surprise shift of power when Alexander I died under mysterious causes in Taganrog, only seventy-five versts from Rostov-on-Don. There were whispers that he tired of playing emperor and faked his death, fading into anonymity in the mountains and passing his rule to his younger brother, mockingly called *the Gendarme of Europe, the Russian Haman*, that reactionary, regressive, Nikolai I, *tfu tfu tfu!*

This Nikolai I unfortunately wasn't killed in the Decembrist revolt. The day before he was set to ascend to the throne after settling the score with those insubordinate generals, he turned to consolidate his power and continue his family legacy of ousting liberals and crushing minorities.

The other crime the so-called Rabinovich was guilty of was being Jewish. If that's not obvious from the assumed birth name, it should be noted that he wasn't a pious Jew. Far from it. Not that he outwardly rejected his faith, but he didn't make any effort to maintain his practice. Perhaps his parents were more observant, but the so-called Rabinovich, from the few footprints he left, didn't visit the synagogue or learning halls. His feet went to the lumber yards and the piers, the local saloons and the forest.

But still, when Nikolai I—*tfu tfu tfu!*—sent the *Ustav rekrutskoi povinnosti*, the law stated that every Jew between twelve and twenty-five had to serve twenty-five years in the army, and if they married, their offspring, as children of Russian soldiers, became the patrimony of the military and were destined to attend the *kantonistskie uchebnye zavedenia* cantonist institution for children. This curse, put on him and tens of thousands of others from the lowest rungs of Jewish society, was irreversible. Towns all across the Pale of Settlement became struck with terror and tumult. Families married off their twelve-year-old boys. Parents starved their children so they would be so malnourished, they would be discharged. Mothers would cut off their children's index finger—if he couldn't shoot, he wouldn't be sent to the front lines.

Still, each community had to pay up and give their share of Jewish youth. Local communal leaders composed draft lists of those who had the means, money, or influence, the tax-paying middle-class families, to buy their way out of this martial life sentence. They were considered "useful Jews." But those "non-useful" Jews—single men, the poor, beggars, outcasts, orphans, heretics, and idlers—were destined to be cannon fodder on the battlefield of the north caucuses, in the forests of northern Europe, the first to charge the hills of Crimea. Of course, they wouldn't go willingly, so the *khapers*, men from the local community, would kidnap children and relinquish them to the Tsar's army. The *khapers*—Jews turning in Jews—became a thing of infamy and eventually turned into a cautionary tale. *If you don't behave, the khapers will come!*

The so-called Rabinovich might have found it odd that he had to serve under a tsar who despised his people, fight for a society that fought against him. Also, screw some son of a Cossack ordering him around like he was dirt, or sleep in a tent in some Caucasian outpost freezing his bollocks off. No way he was joining that crowd who strutted around in their uniform like they were Napoleon. As far he was concerned, the rank and file were sniffling, servile dogs.

Yet, he wasn't going to fast—no, he was too fond of eating, anything really: big blocks of cheese, barrels of herring, potatoes, fried, boiled, or baked—when he could get them.

His friend went on a fast: he was so skinny that, when the *khapers* came to take him, they had to carry him because he couldn't walk. The *khapers* must've decided that bringing him to the enlistment office would be a waste of their time, so they brought him through a ditch. When so-called Rabinovich heard, he and his friends went to look for him. They found him at the bottom of the ditch licking mud.

He wasn't going to marry his cousin, either—perhaps he had too much integrity to wed out of necessity—and though he examined the blade of his mother's butcher knife, he wasn't going to cut off his index finger. After all, you don't know if you *will* have to shoot someone at some point.

The only way to escape this fate was to walk away. At seventeen or eighteen, the so-called Rabinovich fled his home in Rostov-on-Don in the dead of night, leaving everything and everyone behind—including his name.

He dressed as an old beggar (his mother fashioned him a beard from sheep's wool) and began walking from village to village, hopping on and off boats going up and down the river, sleeping in barns and ditches. He, too, licked mud to get his calcium fix.

MET poem 3

Shy Watson

underdressed
beneath the gleeking sky
in line at the metropolitan
museum of art thinking
i should have microdosed
a makeshift bodega umbrella
barely guarding my brains
i invite the members
of "boys DM"
but it's too late
i stand in the rain
until eventually
i belong
on public wifi inside
i feel almost
nothing uterine anguish
moderate envy
in gallery 539
a house a home
to escape into
priorities, like everything
shifting
to the esteemed
jack & belle linsky:
youve made it into a poem

youve made it into the MET
with your trove of belongings
i fantasize
about giving my brother
the life i wish id had
at his age & beyond
thru parental diplomacy
thru money earned by
undisclosed means
i sport "eleventh hour"
spritzed on my wrists
& stare unblinking
at two opposing portraits
of gertrude stein
the coat room: my mother
seadeep & smoldering
the lights all candles
beauty as if
never before
ben lerner reverberates
thru my brain
saying things like
"anachronistic"
i attempt evocation
when i tweet
marital transgressions
is the most beautiful phrase
in the english tongue
standing beneath
a formidable sculpture
perseus chopped off
medusa's head

pass it on

(i peer into a work
not dissimilar to
a doll house
& i think
I believe
in every god
I believe
in every thing)

on the walk home
i feel fond of the florist
on Fulton Street
as i imagine eradicating
all ceremonial gestures
it is windy as shit
for a moment i am gripped
by the fear that
i had somehow
left my journal
at the coffee shop
in high contrast
with bright foreground
a knife pressed to
my throat
syrup viscosity
blood rush
coursing thru me
the sun shines in
at five o'clock
in my past life

i was a painting
scared of nothing
but the dark

Maybe They Don't Fuck Each Other

Nicholas Rys

Hello Tristian,

I was so pleased that my email found you amongst the tide of anonymous submissions you must receive on a daily basis. And yes, I'm glad you agree—I think this would make a fascinating deep dive for your podcast, and potentially YouTube channel, too.

I've known Chuck and Charlie Wagner for several years. In fact, I grew up across the river from their trailer park. I was a few years ahead of them in grade school, until they dropped out in seventh grade.

I'm so excited to talk to you about the TrailerParkTwitterTwins. The story has a lot of potential. The juxtaposition and razor's-edge difference between trailer-trash culture and Internet culture— the Warholian conceptions of contemporary fame—the fleeting Tibetan-Sand-Art nature of the Internet and how it pertains to a New Ephemeral Cultural Moment. What I'm saying is it crosses the goddamn cultural divide!

No one was more surprised than me to read the twins' interview in *Vice*. When I saw that *New York Magazine* said their art "manages to both embody and comment on the contemporary mode of media consumption in our digitally saturated age"—that they "truly transcended classification," well, I barely got the words out to my two dogs, Howler and Ripper, before I laughed like hell.

But I'm getting distracted. You very kindly returned my email because you wanted to know more about them. Something you couldn't find through Google. Well, there are some pretty nasty rumors about those two floating around, and I wouldn't doubt if most of them were true.

They talk openly in interviews about sharing a bed in their mom's trailer, and the art doesn't exactly hide their conditions. The question becomes how much of it is a put-on, and how much of it is true. Everyone knows that weird sells in the art world. When they didn't show up at their art show in Chelsea because, according to a statement posted online, they *had to take care of their mom who just got out of the hospital from a drug overdose,* it was just raw enough for you coastal elites, but everyone around here knows Rita Wagner never touched drugs a day in her life.

Of course, I'm the only son of a bitch in this town that reads *New York Magazine* or keeps up with art or culture, but if you were to ask anyone in Alma if Rita was in the hospital for a drug overdose last February, they'd laugh you right out of town.

I wager most folks here don't even know the twins have a following in the art world or online, and don't give a goddamn to hear about it. They just know Chuck and Charlie as Rita's kids who probably fuck each other.

It all started back in fifth or sixth grade when a boy tried to kiss Charlie on the playground. When Chuck heard, he stabbed the kid in the leg with scissors during indoor recess, said he'd kill him if he ever touched his sister again.

After that, Chuck and Charlie skipped school a lot. The principal would find them in the school attic from time to time—reading picture books to each other and doing God knows what else. Sometimes they'd sneak into the movies at the Westwood Plaza Theatre or walk over to Stutzman playground and just sit under the basketball hoop, never with a ball.

Later, their mom couldn't take all the rumors and pulled them out of school for good. She was a nervous wreck, but never a drug user, or a drinker. She worked at the Dollar General during the day and as a cleaning lady at nights and tutored them when she could so they could get their GED.

But to tell you the truth, Windsor, she did become something of an eccentric. It's nothing new in these parts. Everyone felt bad for the whole lot of them, but never bad enough not to make a quick joke about how those twins obviously fuck each other. It's like that around here. You know, A*t least we're not as bad as the Wagners.*

Maybe that last part was irresponsible. Maybe they don't fuck each other. Maybe, even though they have that photo series where they're in their underwear, prancing around in a kiddie pool filled with cigarettes and tube televisions, and maybe even though they make those videos where they get stoned as hell and roll around in bed and read cut-up poetry to each other in their underwear, it's all a put on. But it doesn't matter, does it? Everyone thinks it's what they do, so they might as well just do it.

Maybe this piece is bigger than Chuck and Charlie. Maybe it's about the Internet or regionalism or something. All I know is that I appreciate you taking an interest in me. Taking an interest in what I have to say. Let's set up a time to talk on the phone and maybe work a way for you to come down here and take a look around. Maybe even meet the twins. Anyway, at the very least I'd love to buy you a beer and tell you more.

All my best –
J. Abraham Crews

prince died for fem bois

Cyree Jarelle Johnson

I said I only want to fuck the taste out of your mouth & I meant it as a furnace. I meant burn manhood down in button up crop tops. I mean burn it down H O U S E Q U A K E like angering Prince as aunty the one with money & two separate couch sets. The one in the front room & its flecks of floral sweats choked in plastic. It squeezes my ass, bites my thighs stinging nettles, but it's hers so I must comply. She glides in on her icy boundaries, says the plastic one is for company. Family is a kind of company. Manhood: the dirty fingers sliding into our plotted eternity. I'll burn every uncovered couch set for you my prince, my aunt, my queen. When I find it I will kill manhood with fire — it is a tick that poisons our infinity. Purposeless, nasty & cruel. Faggotry is the way to nurture the fire. Faggotry is also the way to snuff the fire to steam of memory. Even a tick has purpose — to be devoured by peacocked majestics beating their oiled wings in miraculous flight & we are still fucking. Still thinking of fem princeliness coronated by queenliness. Crown placed, sword sworn by auntie. Watching ticks pop on the match.

Ariel Francisco

An Insomnia Poem

Night nails stars into
the darkening sky
like a father fixing
a roof post-storm
as his son watches
with tiny curiosity—
I can almost hear
the hammering,
ear against the pillow.

Ha, This One's About Insomnia Too

My bed is a godless church
yet I still pray there every night.
Am I a fool? I can almost hear
other worshippers in their far-
off corners, the small breath
of their hands unclasping.

Two Insomniacs On A Sunday Night

Whoever wanders
the alley drags such
heavy feet, as though
shackled by all the
world's unslept hours.

Found Haiku While Reading Aimé Césaire

The only thing in
the world that's worth beginning:
the end of the world.

On Nothing

Rachel Allen

The extract below is from a longer work of fiction, itself tentatively titled "Badlands."

There was never nothing; nothing never begat nothing. That was my first belief, though. Above all, I believed in the abyss from which I'd emerged. The miraculous product of a void multiplied by another. To divide a limitless field, I set a camera on my shoulder. A doubling device containing nothing became my center. From two zeroes (my camera and the void I set it on) came one two: the image proved the existence of an original something. And the two showed three: the three-ness of two is as inevitable as the two-ness of one.

For years after he died, X appeared in my dreams, always at least twice-removed from his self and mine. Once by the usual warp of sleep, which the living are able to dissolve by wakeful reacquaintance, then again by death, not so easy to overcome. In the dreams he was crisp in color and form, even when *he* was not himself. (Often the case with dreamed-bodies, which attach to names and personages not by physiognomy but some other principle, as if in dreaming we pare others to their essences, and pair them back to dreamed-forms accordingly.) The picture verged on hyperreality, but without threat of overdrawing or obfuscation, which are axes of the same uncanny: horror, when the putatively inorganic approaches life; recoil, as it encroaches on the illusion of irreplaceability. X, though, came through without error, the essence I understood as his beaming back at me as if unmediated. He was hi-def, I'm sure of it, and yet when I returned to the dreams, later, they were inevitably altered. Whatever recording device turns on overhead to capture the dream as distinct from its making interferes in the process: the dreams came back to me softened, shot with vaseline on the lens where before they'd been crystalline. Tarkovsky dreams, working light through gauze and vapor, displacing the whole experience, and color-correcting it in sepias: my memory and my dreaming mind torn between reviving X and recasting him as memory.

In a manifesto outlining my position, I discovered an obsession with taxonomizing the empty. At first I sought excisions, emptiness after the fact. Dreams of X afforded me access to an otherwise unavailable beloved, but only by distorting X's person, which I wished not to know was only the detritus of my own. Even within the dreams I found memories implanted, embedded: I would dream a surface dream of dining with X and in the background of my dream-mind would be a memory, not from life or dreamed within the dream, but a visually unrealized backstory.

I wished for the courage of Orpheus, for the will to reunion at the expense of memory, to embrace and live within the unmakeable movie my voided mind suggested, fuck it all, but in truth I was more like Hamlet, mad with grief and misrecognition but only to a point. In addition to the inventions of X's alternate lived experiences (wherein he was Eusebius or Antinous or some Japanese baseball legend), there were the dreams of dying, the long, liminal state of animal being as well as the exact moment of finitude. The worst of these included a subsequent return to death: X would die, in his bedroom or the dreamed-analogue to that hospital-bed where he really did draw final breath, and I would be both gutted and glib and then shortly thereafter encounter him anew as a guest at his own funeral.

His return was not cause for celebration: within the dreams, he was a fellow mourner, not unlively in his carriage, but quite plainly on the verge of a second demise. He is resurrected, only to be dying and then dead all over again.

Waking from such dreams, I experienced sincere pangs of sympathy for the Gospel actors. How much pleasure could there have been in Christ's return, if it was only going to be followed by another, imminent departure? But then their undead was a poor zombie. The truly undead do not perform for an audience in history, as prophets must. Like X they are too ravenous for life to be anything but undiscriminating in their forms.

Gabriel Kruis

    Meanwhile
in el mal pais, leaned out
on mucinex, mixing
dexy cocktails in the
haloed pharmacy
of the car, M
rides shotgun, our
dad at the wheel,
cruising dazed
and feverish
down the highway
between Gallup
and Grants, It's here,
where the sky
is clear
under a spray
of stars, that I
lose them, Where
magnetics go
awry in the lava
fields and the
compass
tilting on the
dash, idles,
then whirrs,
as if moved
by an invisible
hand, Where

the signal goes
under in a wash
of static and M
reaches up
to scan the dial,
country to metal,
Turns it up
when Slipknot
comes on, then
watches her smoke
flare and loom
the domelight,
before it's whisked
out the window
when she flicks
her cigarette
onto the high-
way spinning away
behind her,

                              "I think she likes it,"

my dad tells that 1st night,
standing in the doorway
while I'm in bed,

                              "M, I mean, Playing
                              apothecary, Grinding
                              the pills, Mixing up
                              the syrups,"

        And its this scene
he paints, I play back
in my head when I'm
back at my desk,
staring out from

the 13th floor
at the skyline
shimmering like ice
un-melting, as if
another world
might break through
the mirage heat,
but when I turn
back to the
screen, I know
its no good
reading Guy Debord
when it's clear
how fucked we
are, and watch
instead the wind
map in the shape
of the States
C's sent, with all
its interlocking
patterns and whorls
rendered in real-
time, and I feel,
if only briefly,
the breeze that
rocks the Civic,
where it picks up
on the other side
of the Valley of
Horses, dad jerk
the wheel, Steering
us back from

the rumble
strip, Exhaling
a crimped coke-can's
worth of smoke,
While in the back-
seat J, M's boy-
friend, and his
cousin, Z, play
guitar, inventing
a kind of reservation
slowcore, trading
doped licks of Iron
Maiden, Jimi Hendrix,
Megadeth, B.B.
King, and King
Crimson,

And it accumulates
details as the days go
by, and follows me
home when after work
exhausted but un-
able to sleep, I lay
awake flipping
through AM call-in
shows, night
preachers, conspiracy
theorists, ufologists,
bleeding-edge
therapists, and
actual scientists,
discussing, station

to station, abduction,
resurrection, then
"transgenerational
hauntings," in which
sublimated
psychic material
or "phantoms,"
as they would have it,
pass through the parent's
DNA into the child's
own subconscious,

                  "A residual trauma,

the expert says,

                  "works like a ventriloquist,
                  like a stranger within
                  the subject's own mental
                  topography,"

    My dad my age on
leave from the army,
dissipated on acid,
under the inevitable
stars, on the cliffs
of Big Sur, M's
mother, mother
of 13, pregnant,
with her first
by the age M is
now, and M due
this November,
stripped of her
culture by people
like us, working

doubles at Sonic
and Denny's for
less than a living
wage, on the dole,
as they say, her
medical expenses
covered by her
"Native blood,"
as if it were enough,
it sounds like science
fiction, over-
determined, what
it means for either
of us, I know its
real, and there's
a faint dissolving
light I listen for
between the words
as I search for
sleep, no longer
visible, stretched
out to radiowaves
now, it procedes
from and permeates
the cosmos, a kind
of non-quiet, oceanic
nothing, The Big
Bang attenuated
to static, we pick up
as tee vee snow,
and it obscures
the voices, the

images I fall
asleep imagining,
wake up to
the fugue of, play
back again on
the way back
to work and on
my lunch breaks,
A kind of familial
"Thelma and Louise"
in which we fuck up
the boys who've
raped her and suffer
together the
consequences of laws
that will never
protect her, And
when I need
a break, I get up
from my desk,
take the elevator
down and walk
the 7 minutes
to the park, Outside
the Bonne Vie
boulangerie, half-
catatonic in the heat,
a group of mothers
eat gelato, drink
Perrier, waiting
for their daughters
lounging on the red

carpet staircase
of the Dominican
Academy down
the street, and
when I reach
the park I lay back
on the rocks
and replace the sun
with blood, Listening
for it behind
my eyes,
            A tide
lapping in the pulse
at my neck, An artery
delicate as a shell
under my
thumb, Keeping
time,
        Just enough
to read a poem
or two, and 15
minutes later,
I put my heart
back, tuck my shirt
in, and feel stretch-
marks like seams
of raw silk
above each
hip,
        This body,
This cinema of the
meanwhile, it's a

hyperspace of
memory and
nerves I travel
through to get
to you, And so,
when I catch a cold
I eat too much
mucinex, popping pills
out of the foil
as I walk
to the subway
at 60th and Lex,
sweating and washing
them down
with XXX Vitamin
Water   to induce
a fever that's lucid
and dry like pulling
sheer cloth across
my face, as crystals
and storms
of crystals, form
in my lungs
so that by the time
I'm home
I'm coughing up
clots, and yet
I eat 4 more
and then 4 more
till my organs
hurt, It's stupid
I know, as if

consanguinity
could be achieved
through narcosis,
this ersatz
quanta, still
it's miraculous
at least, how
they clear
the sinuses,
how, as if they
existed in
another country,
my hands become
outliers to me
when I sit down again
to write this
poem,

         In the week
I was back before the bank
foreclosed on our home,
everything was in perfect
disorder with the
symbolic precision
of a nightmare, My huge
family, the straw bale
house my father built,
mostly empty, I was
sleeping in my parents
old room, dad in L's,
M in C's, while the
rest of the beds
lay vacant, On the 2nd
night we stayed up
late smoking out
of M's favorite pipe,
a metal-head's
novelty shaped
like a devil's
claw making
the "a-ok" gesture,
Drawing from
the wrist, schwag
packed like hot
stigmata in the
palm, this sonata-
form dubstep
piece J had
composed blaring
on the laptop,

ending in a montage
of every laugh
Mark Hamill
ever laughed
as The Joker
in "Batman:
The Animated
Series," and I
found myself
trying to imagine
where I was
when they were
out there, leaned
out on mucinex,
driving through
the badlands,
hanging out
after a poetry
reading, probably,
2 hours of
"Cinema of the
Present," maybe,
or at AWP locked
in the Harvard
Advocate coat closet,
smoking out the
window where D
and JT, seemed
trapped in this
möbius strip
dialectic on
privilege and

the place of the
other in the crisis
of infinite worlds,
pausing only
briefly to survey
the room for
other intoxicants,
at which point T
offered poppers
and DD set to work
rolling a joint on the
filing cabinet, while
JT kept repeating,

"There is no 'we,' There
is no 'we,' D, don't
you get it, That's the
thing, There's no 'we,'"

This, a brief forever
looped by virtue of
the poppers, and M

"there is no 'we'"

is rolling a joint even
slower than DD,
on our kitchen table,
where that spring, she

"there is no 'we'"

sat filling milk jugs with
knock-off Robitussin, Jolly
Ranchers, Mucinex,
and Oxycodone, and later, me

"there is no 'we'"

and my dad talked about

how the kids ate pills
till their kidneys hurt,
tripping in superposition,

        "there is no 'we'"

shoplifting and mixing,
driving back and forth
to barter for schwag,
till the huffed drunk flange

        "there is no 'we'"

of Pure Gold isobutyl
nitrites, PBR and zinfandel,
resolved into a pre-hung
over hum and the leaden echo

        "there is no 'we'"

goes quiet, the fluorescent
lights go out, and it's
morning and M's frying
donuts when I walk
into the kitchen, a clear
pool of lard in the skillet,
a bag of Blue Bird flour
on the counter beside
her, and even though it's
early and I haven't had my
coffee, she asks me
if I believe in demons
and I say, "I don't know,
I guess so," but did I
mean it, thinking
of Rattray,

        "Of poets,
        according to Jahiz,

the best are possessed
by genies, the next-best
by friendly Demons,
the average by fallen
angels, and the bad
by the Devil himself,"

Or was I only moving
the conversation along,

"I mean think about it,"

she says,

"we all have one, Mom
has one, Dad has one
I have one, You have one,"

And it only strikes
me, waiting later that week
for the plane to take me
back to Brooklyn, later
that week, that this is
what others mean
when they say, "soul,"
and from where I sat
on the tarmac, the
thunderheads lit up
in the permanent
revolutions of the sun,
looked like guillotines
tempered in honey,
while the essence
of the air was red,
as it is each evening
at that hour,
slowed, the speed

of light stopped-
gold, when
nothing
seems to happen
all at once,
and downpours
sublime
in the heat
above our
heads,

ARTISTS AND WRITERS

Rachel Allen is a writer from New York and North Carolina. Her work has been in *Best American Experimental 2018, 3:am, Full Stop, Guernica*, and *The Fanzine*. She is an editor at *Guernica* and at *Asymptote*. In 2019, she was in residence with the Tulsa Artist Fellowship.

Phil Anderson has an MFA in fiction from Columbia University, where he also taught undergraduate creative writing. He is currently working on a collection of stories and a novel. He lives in New Haven with his partner and two cats.

Brendan Burdzinski lives and works in New York, NY. Recent exhibitions include Grand Slam, Geary Contemporary (2017), Annual Group Show, Wood Pile (2016), Cold Open Verse, presented by Blonde Art Books & Poet Transmit, Knockdown Center (2016), and One Night Stand, Duty Free Gallery (2016). He also participated in the Los Angeles, CA exhibition Snap to Grid, LACDA (2015). Curatorial projects include Postures: Sophie Hirsch, Duty Free Gallery (2016). He received a BA in Photojournalism from California State University, Long Beach. His work has been featured in *Cultured Magazine, Dazed, Muse, Office, Puss Puss, T, Vanity Fair* and others.

Naomi Falk is a writer and editor who lives in Bushwick. Her writing fixates on art, intimacy, and the ways in which we engage and disconnect our sensory perceptions. She works at The Museum of Modern Art, is co-founder of *NAUSIKÂE*, is an editor for Archways Editions, and is a founding member of HOLE NYC. Her work has been published by *BOMB Magazine*, *Black Sun Lit*, Ki Smith Gallery, and others.

Katie Foster is a poet, artist, and translator based in Brooklyn, New York. Her writing concerns itself with dreams, notions of home, animals, and what sits just beyond the reach of language. She has lived her professional life in service of literature. Past positions include Bookseller & Big Tent Reading Coordinator at The Raven Bookstore in Lawrence, Kansas, Graduate Student Teacher of Literary Arts at Brown University, and Editorial Intern at *BOMB Magazine* in Brooklyn.

Ariel Francisco Henriquez Cos is the author of *A Sinking Ship is Still a Ship* (Burrow Press, 2020), *All My Heroes Are Broke* (C&R Press, 2017) which was named one of the 8 Best Latino Books of 2017 by Rigoberto Gonzalez, and *Before Snowfall, After Rain* (Glass Poetry Press, 2016). Born in the Bronx to Dominican and Guatemalan parents, he was raised in Miami and completed his MFA at Florida International University. He now lives in Brooklyn and is completing a master's in literary translation. He was named one of the Five Florida Writers to Watch in 2019 by *The Miami New Times*.

Kelly Gallagher is a filmmaker, animator, and Assistant Professor of Film at Syracuse University. Her award-winning films and commissioned animations have screened internationally at venues including: the Museum of Modern Art, The National Gallery of Art, Sundance Film Festival, the Smithsonian Institution, and Ann Arbor Film Festival. She's presented solo programs of her work at institutions including: UnionDocs, the Wexner, University of Michigan, and UC Santa Cruz, among others. Kelly enthusiastically organizes and facilitates film workshops, camps, and masterclasses for communities and groups of all ages.

Andrew Gibeley is a writer in Brooklyn. Raised in a rural town in Connecticut, much of his poetry derives from his suburban upbringing and the matter-of-fact ennui of everyday life. He graduated cum laude from Hamilton College in 2016 with honors in creative writing, before completing the NYU Summer Publishing Institute which led him to HarperCollins Publishers where he currently spends his days as an assistant publicist for William Morrow. He recently participated in Alex Dimitrov's summer poetry workshop at 92Y.

Cyree Jarelle Johnson is a writer and librarian living in New York City. His first book of poetry *SLINGSHOT* was published by Nightboat Books in 2019. He is currently an Undergraduate Creative Writing Teaching Fellow at Columbia University, where he is also a candidate for an MFA. His work has appeared recently in *The New York Times* and *WUSSY*. He has given speeches and lectures at The White House, The Whitney Museum of American Art, The University of Pennsylvania, The Philadelphia Trans Health Conference, Tufts University, and Mother Bethel AME Church, among other venues. His work has been profiled on PBS News Hour and Mashable. Cyrée Jarelle has received fellowships and grants from Culture/Strike, Leeway Foundation, Astraea Foundation, Rewire.News/Disabled Writers, Columbia University, and the Davis-Putter Scholarship Fund. He is a founding member of The Harriet Tubman Collective and The Deaf Poets Society.

Gabriel Kruis is a New Mexican poet and educator living and writing in Brooklyn. His memoir in verse *Acid Virga* was published in 2020 by Archway Editions. He is a cofounder of Wendy's Subway Reading Room and his work has been published in *A Perfect Vacuum*, *PEN America Poetry Series*, *OmniVerse*, *The Brooklyn Rail*, *Atlas Review*, *Frontier Poetry*, among others.

Shay Lawz is a poet and interdisciplinary artist from Jersey City, NJ. She works at the intersection of text and performance and has presented work at Brown University, RISD, AS220, and Pratt Institute. Her writing appears or is forthcoming in *Aster(ix), Winter Tangerine*, and *McSweeney's Quarterly Concern*. She is a graduate of Brown University's MFA program and has received fellowships/residencies from Jack Jones Literary Arts, Cave Canem, and CAAPP (University of Pittsburgh). She is a 2019-2020 Digital Studies fellow at Rutgers-Camden and teaches at Pratt Institute in the department of Humanities and Media Studies. She lives in Brooklyn, NY.

Etan Nechin is an Israeli-born journalist, author, and online editor for *The Bare Life Review*, a journal of immigrant and refugee literature. Twitter: @Etanetan23

Kwame Opoku-Duku is a Ghanaian-American poet and fiction writer. He is the author of *The Unbnd Verses* (Glass Poetry Press, 2018), and his work is featured in *The Virginia Quarterly Review, The Kenyon Review, BOMB, Apogee, The Literary Review, Bettering American Poetry,* and other publications. Kwame lives in New York City, where he is an educator, and along with Karisma Price, he is a founding member of the Unbnd Collective. Kwame is an associate poetry editor for *BOAAT Journal,* and he curates the reading series *Dear Ocean.*

Chunbum Park, also known as Chun, is a BFA Fine Arts student attending the School of Visual Arts in NYC. He was born in Seoul, South Korea, in 1991. He grew up in Mokpo and came to the United States in 2000 to study English and attend school. After finishing high school at the Montgomery Bell Academy in Nashville, he briefly attended various schools including University of Rochester, Bergen Community College, Rhode Island School of Design, and Art Students League of NY. He is finally set to receive his BFA in 2020 and hopes to go to a graduate school afterwards.

Joseph Rathgeber is an author, poet, high school English teacher, and adjunct professor from New Jersey. His novel *Mixedbloods* was published by Fomite in 2019. His story collection is *The Abridged Autobiography of Yousef R. and Other Stories* (ELJ Publications, 2014). His work of hybrid poetry is *MJ* (Another New Calligraphy, 2015). He is the recipient of a 2014 New Jersey State Council on the Arts Fellowship (Poetry) and a 2016 National Endowment for the Arts Creative Writing Fellowship (Prose). He is a member of the National Writers Union UAW Local 1981/AFL-CIO, Federation of Adjunct Faculty AFT Local 6025, and the NJEA.

Nicholas Rys is a writer and college instructor who lives in Syracuse, New York. His fiction has appeared in or is forthcoming from *Hobart, Heavy Feather Review, BULL, the Antioch Review*, and others. He has an MFA in fiction from Bowling Green State University.

Andréa Stella (she/her/hers) teaches Writing for Engineering at the City College of New York and researches how to de-center whiteness in STEM writing composition for her PhD at the Graduate Center. She spent a decade running a syringe exchange in the East Village.

Shy Watson wrote *Cheap Yellow* (CCM, 2018), co-founded *blush lit*, & is now working on a novel. find more of shy's work at places like *New York Tyrant, The Rumpus*, & *[PANK]*. follow @formermissNJ on twitter for updates.

MORE FROM ARCHWAY EDITIONS

Ishmael Reed – *The Haunting of Lin-Manuel Miranda*
Unpublishable (edited by Chris Molnar and Etan Nechin)
Gabriel Kruis – *Acid Virga*
Erin Taylor – *Bimboland*
NDA: An Autofiction Anthology (edited by Caitlin Forst)
Mike Sacks – *Randy*
Mike Sacks – *Stinker Lets Loose*
Paul Schrader – *First Reformed*
Brantly Martin – *Highway B: Horrorfest*
Stacy Szymaszek – *Famous Hermits*
cokemachineglow (edited by Clayton Purdom)
Ishmael Reed – *Life Among the Aryans*
Alice Notley – *Runes and Chords*

Archway Editions can be found at your local bookstore or ordered directly through Simon & Schuster.

Questions? Comments? Concerns? Send correspondence to:

> Archway Editions
> c/o powerHouse Books
> 220 36th St., Building #2
> Brooklyn, NY
> 11232